HIDING AMONGST ONESELF

ABRIEL BORDELON

CONTENTS

PART I

SWAYING TIDES

Humans are like chameleons, using camouflage to blend into their surroundings to avoid danger. However, humans seem to utilize that ability to harm others. You think you know someone you've grown up with, then they go and stab you in the back without a second thought. Sharing secrets with others only causes pain; my brother taught me that. Albeit, not for me to better myself as a person, but rather to exploit what he saw as a flaw. The sound of my father hurriedly stomping up the stairs paired with shouts of my name plagued my brain. The sound of my bedroom door slamming against the wall as my father flung it open, surprisingly the door hinges held the door in place. The searing pain from each smack and whip from my father's belt left red marks and welts in its wake as I rushed to escape this purgatory. The brother who had taken our bond that accumulated over many years was thrown to the waste side as he stood at the door. All he did in response to the situation was pointing and mocking me for being a "pussy", instead of fighting for his little brother to stay in the home we were once raised in. From watching cartoons to popping open bottles of alcohol eventually accumulated to a night consumed with dread, hatred, and self-hatred.

Families are supposed to have your back, that's what the media always portrayed. However, my family threw me out like a pile of trash, as if I were a stranger. The ones who raised me and brought me into this world to become someone who would benefit society and develop into an independent human.

The world around me spun and contorted into a nauseating swirl of confusion, the room was pitch black as if I was being sucked into a void of never-ending darkness. The only sound was the sound of myself hyperventilating, anxiety surging through my veins. Sweat was dripping from my forehead, soaking my pillow, and clothing. Shaky breaths escaped my lungs in quick bursts as my body attempted to fill them with air to calm these nerves, only leading me to feel suffocated. That nightmare has been plaguing my mind since the day I escaped from that hell only a couple of months ago. Daniel was still asleep beside me; all I could see was his blonde hair poking out from our shared blanket. Reaching out to brush my hair only to stop upon realizing the extent of my tremors.

"Fuck." Cursing quietly under my breath at the hindering revelation once again. Looks like I'd need to use that damn medicine again, it didn't help I forget to take it consistently. The thoughts raced in my mind, contemplating swallowing my pride and going back to sleep or taking the plunge. A slight shift under the blankets caught my attention as Daniel's sleeping form adjusted to get more comfortable under our shared blanket. The last thing I wanted was to make him worry again, he's always there whenever despair envelops me. However, waking him up would only hinder him tomorrow, as he had an important job meeting with his boss in the morning. Slowly lifting the blanket off rummaging in the darkness for some warm slippers and making my way to the bathroom was more of a challenge than expected. The old floorboards creaked with every step I took; my movement was sluggish, and my thoughts were muddled and cloudy. Dizziness clouded my head as I tried to alleviate the pounding by shutting my eyes to shield them from the impending bright lights from the bathroom. It felt like an hour had passed before I made it to our bathroom. The sounds from neighboring residents could be faintly heard through the thin apartment walls; sounds of footsteps and faint snoring could be heard as I reached for a towel to wipe the sweat from my pale face. The sink water was cold when I splashed it on my face, we must have forgotten to pay the water bill again, no hot shower for either of us tonight.

As I opened the door to our medicine cabinet, a voice snapped me out of my dazed state.

"What are you doing?"

Daniel questioned my hunched figure as he entered the bathroom alongside me. Damn it, the one thing I did not want to do, I ended up doing anyway.

"Sorry babe, had that dream again," I answered as I rifled through the medicine cabinet in search of something to relieve me of my impending panic attack once again. The best thing to do when you have night terrors is to drown it out with alprazolam, every functioning human relies on pills to cure their sorrows right?

"Aaron, don't take that." Daniel never approved of how often I relied on medications. Side effects are just part of the deal, like selling my soul to the devil. Feel better at night, then feel like shit in the morning. The vicious cycle of prescriptions was something Daniel was adamant about helping me through with natural remedies. I love him with all my heart for that, but it will not help me now.

"Sorry, but I won't be able to sleep if I don't." I yawned; this only made him frown at me in disappointment. That expression does not suit him, seeing him like that always weakened my resolve to continue to argue back. Daniel brushed his fingers through his long blonde hair and huffed in annoyance at the lack of response.

"Relying on pills is not going to solve all your problems. Let me help you," Daniel said in an exasperated tone as he yanked the medicine bottle out of my hands.

Daniel put the alprazolam back in the cabinet and pulled me out of the bathroom as I groaned in frustration at my lack of willingness to fight his attempts at helping me once more.

"I do not want you losing sleep because of my issues. I can handle it."

Daniel stopped walking as he turned his head in my direction to look back at me. His eyes showed his disapproval once again as our eyes connected.

"I know you do not like worrying me, Aaron. However, when you push me away it only makes me even more concerned about you. Just let me do this now and we will go back to bed, okay?"

Trusting others has never been my forte. However, when it came to Daniel, he was the only one I felt at peace with. I have snapped out of my thoughts once again at the sound of a click from his unlocking the patio sliding door.

Suddenly, we were on the bedroom balcony, the night sky filled with thousands of tiny stars littered the sky. The view was so beautiful it felt like it was a painting that jumped off a canvas and into the sky.

"Just take in some fresh air, I'll be back in a second," Daniel said as he went back into the bedroom. The air was relaxing, albeit cold, but it was comforting. Breathing in the night air always gave me a sense of freedom, like nothing could hurt me.

Suddenly, my body was engulfed in a comforting warmth, two arms coiled around my waist, pulling me into a sturdy chest. "Thought you would want your blanket. Would not want you catching a cold now, would I?" Daniel whispered in a soothing voice behind my ear as I leaned against the patio railing. Daniel had wrapped us both in that silly pink blanket he gifted me for Valentine's Day. The blanket was one of the standard fluffy seasonal blankets you could find at any Walmart, covered in red hearts and everything. It may have been incredibly corny, but the admiration behind the gift never failed to make my heart flutter. His hugs always felt the best too, like the comforting warmth of hot cocoa during a winter evening next to a fireplace. "Doesn't this feel better than choking down pills?" Daniel asked in a teasing voice as I rolled my eyes at his questioning look.

Reluctantly, I nodded my head in agreement, removed one of his hands from my waist, and laced our fingers together, squeezing his hand affectionately.

"Yes, it does," I replied in a tired voice with an exasperated sigh, yawning after I finished.

"Do you want to talk about what you saw?" Daniel questioned as he readjusted the blanket to fit around the both of us better.

Sighing in defeat, I rested my head against Daniel's shoulder, nodding my head reluctantly in agreement. "You know how it starts."

PART II

FOREIGN CONNECTIONS

Snow fell from the gray cloudy sky, there was a slight fog that day.

Resting my head against my brother's car door, staring down at the half-empty bottle of alcohol in my hands. "Nate, can we talk?"

Nate tossed the glass bottle of alcohol at the brick wall behind us, shattering it in an instant as he trudged over to me. "Spill."

Taking in a breath to compose myself, I watched the little cloud of condensation escape me as an exhale slipped past my lips.

"I've been feeling weird lately."

Nate gave a confused look and reached inside his car for another drink. "I would imagine, you're normally conked out by now," Nate emphasized his statement by pointing at the bottle I was holding.

"Shut the hell up!" I laughed out while playfully shoving his shoulder as his laughter continued. "No seriously, it's hard to explain," I muttered, rubbing my gloved fingers against the rim of the bottle in thought. "Do you remember when we threw that party? The one you invited Daniel to?"

Nate paused, popping the cap off of his bottle in thought as he took a swig and silently pondered. "Right, I remember! When we broke the TV with a ping pong racket!"

A chuckle escaped me as I combed my fingers through my shaggy brown fringe out of my green eyes. "Yes, that one. Something else happened during that party." The breath in my body was caught in my throat as I anxiously whipped my phone out of my gray sweater pocket and showed the screen to Nate. "I haven't shown this to anyone. I want this to stay between the two of us, brother to brother."

The expression on Nate's face changed to a perplexed look when his eyes met the phone screen, many emotions melding into one, none that I could discern at the moment. I lowered the phone and analyzed the photo, I could still feel the butterflies fluttering in my stomach from the mere memory of what transpired, not that even a month ago. The photo I had saved was of Daniel and I kissing; we were both hella drunk that night. Daniel was wearing a black and white striped long-sleeve shirt, his long blonde hair fell past his shoulders as his left hand fisted into my shoulder-length brown hair.

"Things had gotten a little uh… intense."

Every time I saw that photo, it made me feel something. It was a feeling I'd never felt before. It made my throat feel suffocatingly tight and my chest heavy, although it was a warm and welcoming feeling. Mom and Dad would kill me if they ever found out, they made their opinions about people like me quite evident whenever the discussion came up from the news or people in public. Living in a religious home with strict rules was not an ideal situation for someone like Nate and me. The possible repercussions did not affect me whenever the image of Daniel plagued my mind, the world felt livelier with him. Interacting with the friends made along the way at our many parties made Nate and I realize there was more to life than getting belittled by your parents or arduously studying until the sun arose from the ashes.

We always named our parties when we threw one. Nate and I decided this one would be called "Alcohol Shore." Nate was known to stock up on alcohol, and parties were not an exception. During the planning process of the party, Nate had the bright idea to fill a chocolate fountain with alcohol. Our parents were going out for their anniversary, so what was a better way to celebrate a day without your parents in Ohio? Invite everyone you know and throw a party until the sun comes up!

"Aaron, I got Daniel and a couple of others coming over. Who are you inviting this time?" My green eyes met with Nate's brown eyes with a questioning look. His breath smelled faintly of mint and his clothes had an overbearing amount of cologne. His poorly dyed red and natural brown hair was a mess. He looked like he just rolled out of bed and threw on the first thing he laid eyes on. He wore one of his wrinkled metal band shirts, and his wrists were covered in at least ten rubber bracelets.

"Nate, why are you vaping? The party is starting in an hour, you can't wait?" Nate's face contorted into a childish pout as he took another puff from his vape pen and blew the smoke in my face.

"Careful, you're starting to sound like Dad." The jab I felt in my gut was intense when he said that. I knew he was joking, but it still hurt thinking I could have been similar to our father in any way.

I first grasped onto one of the couch pillows and threw it at him. "Don't say that." Huffing out a breath of frustration while eyeing him with a look of slight disgust. "I'm only inviting Lillie, everyone else is busy."

Nate turned away and picked up a notebook, scribbling down Lillie's name. Lillie was like the little sister I never had. She was innocent and oblivious to the world around her.

"Sweet! She's the one with the massive tits right?"

Grimacing at Nate's crude statement, I threw another pillow at him. That was why he could never keep a girlfriend. Remembering women solely for their physical attributes rather than their personality or their actions. Being brothers helps you pick out the traits in someone, especially the bad ones. At least he's inviting Daniel, it's been a while since we've last hung out.

"While you finish our guest list, let's go buy some Vodka for tonight!"

Nate's fist pumps up into the air out of excitement as he exclaims. Chortling a bit under my breath at his childish antics that never seemed to change, I stood up and tightened my shoelaces.

"Alright, but you're driving okay? We also need to get fruit punch and water while we're there."

Looking over my shoulder only to see Nate had not heard a thing I said. Instead opting to sing a rock song under his breath while lacing his Converse. Doing a finger drum motion after finishing putting his shoes on and making eye contact with me.

"We gotta get chips too! What's that look for?"

The glare was clear to even the blind, he's ignorant of everything but himself. He's an expert at pissing me off even unintentionally. Flipping him my middle finger jokingly before unlocking the front door.

"I said we need to buy *fruit punch* and *water* stupid?"

The drive to the gas station was a short one, the distance was roughly five miles away from our neighborhood. Upon entering, the light from the sun reflected off one of the best human creations, slushie machines. Nothing tastes better during a liquor store trip than artificially flavored drinks, right? As I began filling up a cup someone called out to me.

"Hey Aaron!"

Lille greeted, walking up to me and waving at me, grabbing a cup for herself and looking over each option provided. Dawning wavy red hair, tied up into a neatly done ponytail, a brown jacket with a green scarf covering her nose, and a green skirt alongside leggings.

"Woah you're out here while it is snowing? Are you the same Lillie that I know?"

She begrudgingly ignored the remark, shuffling her way to the coffee to warm up in the arctic tundras these last months. Hurriedly pouring black coffee into her cup, taking a quick sip before barking at me.

"I hate the cold! This is why I stay inside during winter. How am I supposed to monitor the park in this hellish weather?!"

Obnoxiously she sobbed, her shivering ceasing at the profound effect coffee had on her, as she mentions on occasion. Park rangers are tasked to work during cold weather, although she is still new to her job. Environmental work is a passion career for Lillie. Hiking was her biggest hobby, anything outdoors and active. However, the cold was something she disdained. Leaving yards an ominous brown, shedding the colorful green it used to bear. The best way to cheer anyone up would be a surprise.

"Since you're here Lillie, Nate and I came here to buy some party necessities. You're invited to our party tonight if you wanna join."

Lillie's hazel eyes glimmered in silent excitement at her received invite. Setting down her coffee momentarily to properly respond without dropping it. Her parents had quite the habit of sheltering her from anything possibly dangerous. However, they placed some trust in me over time to watch out for her during occasions like these. Being an only child with wealthy parents turned me into an older brother figure for her.

"Yes, that sounds fun! I'll be there in an hour."

Bringing all the necessities to the counter, Daniel was working today and snuck us a favorable discount. Since Daniel was working different jobs like these, it gave us an affordable outlet for alcohol. Now don't get me wrong, we're legally old enough to drink, but liquor ain't cheap in most shops around here.

"So will this be everything for you three?"

Daniel questioned us as he eyed the three of us while bagging our goods. Lillie kindly offered to pay for everyone's things, everything is set in stone. The snacks and beverages are bought, Lillie will be partying with us, and everyone has received their invite. Everyone, except for one last person.

"Hey Daniel, we're going to be throwing a party tonight. You're also invited if you want to join."

The slightest widening of Daniel's eyes did not go missed by my astute eyes. The glimmer of excitement was evident, Daniel would always perform in the band he formed with Nate and their friends. Guitar solos were something he had a fluent ability with. Coming as naturally to him as a fish to water, a passionate musician. Awaiting his offer to perform at our place, my thoughts were interrupted by a warm hand placed atop my own on the counter.

"I must say I'm happy that you're inviting me this time Aaron."

His words sounded like velvet as each one left his lips in a whisper, only for my ears to catch. Daniel's eyes watching mine in anticipation, as if a predator was hunting for prey. The intensity of his gaze made my hand slowly retract in anxiousness and a bit of shyness at the unusual behavior he presented today.

"Good, we always invite you anyway so if you want to play your music tonight feel free."

Foldable tables littered the entire house with alcohol cans scattered atop them; alongside them were chips and dip. We provided soda and water for the sober people; we couldn't leave anyone out on the fun. Lillie wouldn't have agreed to come in the first place if there was only alcohol. Lillie didn't appear too thrilled to be here despite the diverse options we provided. She looked like a child who had their Xbox taken away from them. Her small fists gripped at the end of her mocha skirt, her red hair tied in a bun, and her curly bangs framed her freckled cheeks, giving off an innocent and pure style. She looked more prepared to go hiking up a mountain rather than partying.

"Aaron, I'm going to go dance." Lillie was always a master with the doe-eye puppy dog look.

Feeling my resolve crumbling, I reluctantly got up from the couch. "Lillie, I would prefer you stay close to me tonight, Nate invited some unfamiliar faces."

The pout that formed on her face was evident as her brown eyes formed into angry daggers at the comment. "I appreciate the concern but I'm not a child you know, I can take care of myself!" She annoyingly responded, as if that would quell my suspicions of these people here. Despite her being correct that she is an adult, she still behaves like a child most certainly.

To emphasize the weight behind my words I placed my hands over her shoulders. "No, trust me when I say this, please. Last time I let you do whatever you ended up blackout drunk on the bathroom floor. Your parents and mine were not thrilled in the slightest, including me."

Lillie jumped up from the couch and got close to my face to "intimidate me" into allowing her to do what she wanted. Lillie is the epitome of a spoiled princess, doesn't help her parents are wealthy, and has no backbone when it comes to her desires. Despite the bratty attitude from time to time, she holds a heart of gold and the bravery of a soldier going to war whenever it comes to a challenge.

"Come on Aaron, you know I quit drinking after that night! Plus, I recently earned a purple belt in self-defense class!" The hard exterior of my resolve was crumbling quickly at her constant begging and persistence. Letting out a reluctant sigh, my hands left her shoulders and shook my head in defeat at her antics. "Alright, but don't accept drinks from anyone you don't know, got it?"

Lillie nodded at me and rushed to dance with everyone. I didn't mean to treat her like a child, but I couldn't trust her to be mindful of her surroundings. Being safe is always better than facing the consequences of danger, Nate and I know that better than anyone present. However, I needed to know the limited authority I had over her. Lillie was like the little sister I never had, she held so much innocence and naivety in her that anyone could take advantage of her. Her parents did not help with sheltering her from the evil of the world. However, despite her protests, I adopted the role of her older brother to protect her from the many terrible things that could manipulate her. Nate was one of those people who would most certainly use her naivety against her for his gain. The alcohol and these negative thoughts were only causing my stress, fresh air was due for me to clear these inner demons.

I made my way to the backyard, sat down on the patio in front of the backdoor, and took a deep breath. Loud music made me feel nauseous sometimes, it made me feel on edge, reminding me that we were doing something we shouldn't. Alongside the alcohol, it was not a good combination. The fresh air always made me feel like I was trapped; reminding me how I am forced to live under so many restrictions in this household.

"Hey, why are you out here by yourself?" The sliding glass door shut, and the curtains obscured the view of the chaos inside. A hand began ruffling my hair, I relaxed when I recognized the voice.

"Hey Daniel, you're not going to play beer bong with Nate?"

Daniel sat down next to me and placed his alcohol beside him. "Nah, I saw you come out here and wanted to make sure you were okay." Daniel knew I wasn't as much of a partier as my brother was. The hard-drinking playboy older brother is better at partying than the younger lightweight brother, surprising.

"I just needed some fresh air; the music was starting to bother me."

Daniel laughed at my reply, shaking my shoulder in the process. Daniel was always known as the music guy, so it is understandable. His talent with an instrument honestly made me a bit envious. "You're adorable, you know that?"

My body froze at that, what did he say? Me, adorable? I swallowed nervously and cleared my throat as I attempted to understand what was going on at this moment. "Oh, am I now?" It sounded more like a statement than a question. This was an unusual situation; however, it was not a bad one.

"Yeah, I always thought you were Aaron."

Wait, so he was saying that seriously? "What are you saying? I'm a guy, isn't that weird to say that to another guy?" I questioned him, letting out a nervous chuckle. His face didn't show an ounce of humor or shame, the only thing was his warm inviting smile and his hair gently blowing in the wind.

"Why would that be weird? I don't see you for your gender, I see you for who you are, as Aaron." Daniel confessed in a serious tone, making my heart flutter. My mouth went slightly agape, and I looked away, my face felt flushed in an unbearable heat of embarrassment. That should not be happening, it is snowing out here for God's sake.

Mom and Dad instilled in my brother and I that same-sex relationships were sinful. Why is Daniel speaking like it is not a big deal? I cleared my throat for the second time and focused my eyes on the snow-covered grass.

"You're drunk, Daniel." He pulled me back down as I attempted to go back inside to escape this unfamiliar situation unfolding before me.

"I want to know how you feel, Aaron," Daniel admitted in a soft voice, his cheeks also holding a slight pink tint. I allowed myself to get a good look at his face upon noticing his slightly shy demeanor. His long blonde hair looked as soft as silk and shone like a diamond, his black and white striped long-sleeved shirt fitting nicely over his slim yet nicely built frame, and his ripped acid jeans complimenting his passion for his arts in music perfectly. The thing that stuck out to me the most was his eyes, that striking bright blue that looked right back into mine. Those eyes of his felt like I was being entranced by how much they resembled lapis lazuli gems. I began to relax and shuffled closer to Daniel until our shoulders touched, that single touch of intimacy sending thousands of tingly yet pleasant shocks.

"I'm not entirely sure." Daniel cradled the back of my head and pulled me closer to him. Our foreheads touched, his warm breath fanning my face that smelled of liquor and weed. It felt so warm, so natural. I've never felt something like this with anyone, why with Daniel? "Aaron, I want to try something," Daniel whispered to me as he lifted my chin. The words I wanted to say wouldn't escape me, all I could do was nod my head and close my eyes awaiting what Daniel would do.

That was when it happened, I felt the soft touch of Daniel's lips enclosing mine.

At that moment everything became clear to me. What I was feeling was love, an emotion that felt so foreign yet so comforting. My hand made its way up to Daniel's hair, tugging it like he did with my hair. I didn't want this to end, I felt like I discovered something I never knew was inside of me. It felt like an hour had gone by before Daniel released his grip on my hair and pulled his lips away from me, leaning his forehead against mine again.

"How about now?" Daniel questioned as we both tried to regulate our breathing. Once we caught our breath we sat in silence, basking in the intimacy. "I love you too." Daniel pulled away laughing and ruffled my hair again. "I'm glad, check this out." Daniel showed me his phone screen and my face probably resembled a tomato at that moment.

"Why the hell would you do that?" I questioned in embarrassment as my hands attempted to hide my face at what he had just shown me. It was a picture of us kissing, when did he take that?!

"Aww, don't be shy. I won't show anyone. It will be our little memento from tonight!" Daniel teased. He started laughing again when I smacked his shoulder.

"My parents would kill me if they saw that." Daniel stopped laughing once I said that.

"Oh, you have those kinds of parents, huh?" Daniel stood up and reached his hand out to me, signaling me to get up.

"If they do something you can always reach out to me, okay?"

PART III

RIFT IN THE SNOW

Nate's eyes were trained on the snowy floor underneath us. "You know Mom and Dad would disown you if they knew," Nate stated quietly, almost slipping by me.

Of course, I knew that! They raised us to adopt their hatred and opinions since we were young. Brainwashing us the minute we could even remotely develop the ability to form our own opinions. Raising us to worship and love God and hate anything that went against that. Wouldn't that very mindset go against the teachings he bestowed upon us mortals, to begin with? That part was left forgotten by the brilliant minds of the people who spawned us into this wretched world.

"I know, but this is who I am. I can't hide it forever." I answered. I stood up and dusted the snow off myself, offering a hand to Nate.

When Nate finally looked at me, his eyes held a new emotion in them, something I couldn't discern. It felt like he was looking at a stranger.

However, he still grabbed my hand and stood up.

"Nate, we haven't been following Mom and Dad's teachings as strictly as they would like. I am hoping this is another rule we can break." Nate eyed me one last time and got into his car. "Of course, Aaron, you are my brother after all."

Despite the drive home being quiet, I felt a sense of accomplishment and belonging. The emotional chains that were locked down in my heart felt like they were finally cracking after so long! Nate's expression held one of a curt smile as he glanced at me, quickly returning his gaze to the road. Reaching a handout to place my hand over his on the shift stick to calm pounding in my heart at how vulnerable this whole moment felt.

"We should throw another party soon Nate. I will invite Daniel and I can help you get with Lillie as long as you behave yourself, okay?"

The only response I received was a chuckle from Nate who kept his focus on not killing us while driving. The only sounds heard in the Clayfield household were screaming, banging, and cackling. All I could do was run as fast as my legs could take me, the fear and adrenaline coursing through my veins. Nate went into my room to steal my phone once it was out of my sight and showed our Mom and Dad the photo of Daniel and me. The brother I grew up with my whole life threw me out to the dogs. The brother that broke all the rules alongside me betrayed me to save his ass.

After all the years of not following Mom and Dad's religious traditions and rules changed instantly. The one time my brother wouldn't stand by my side and embraced the toxic grip from our narcissistic sperm donor and baby oven. The rough hands of my father threw me out of the house and slammed the door shut. Snow flew up into the air as I landed on the frozen driveway, the only thing I could feel was numbness all over me. The snow was not what caused this feeling, how was I supposed to feel? Nate, Mother, and Father proved in this instant they never genuinely loved or cared for me. If they had they would have accepted me, this is something I never thought could happen to me. Anger, sadness, shame, regret, and shock were meddling into one horrifically dreadful emotion all at once in my shaken brain. The cold snow was crunching under me when I stood up, letting the snow from above fall over my pathetic form. Leaving me out here with just the skin on my back. Without an understanding of where the next destination to go to or do I let my weak legs take me wherever they lead me to, not bothering to have one last glance of my old home.

Cold was all that was felt as the aimless journey continued, time was left forgotten. Has it been an hour of walking, maybe it's only been a couple of minutes? People walking past me gave fleeting looks at my hunched-over form, face and hands read from the piercing weather. Lifelessly trudging on the sidewalk, a sudden force collided with my body, knocking me to the ground and landing on my sorry ass.

"Watch where you're going asshole!"

The voice sounded like an angry older man; I couldn't care enough to bring my gaze up to check. He probably thought I was a walking corpse, might as well be after today. Once the geezer left, I slowly brought my dead eyes to the sky, it has gotten dark now. However, it looks like I ended up in a familiar spot at least. Worn Retreat was where my legs were guiding me. This was one of the many apartment complexes in our city, particularly housing someone I've had many encounters and interactions with. A couple of parties have been thrown at their place, so the cops know this place just as well as Nate and I.

Ascending one of the couple's squeaky staircases in the building was accompanied by muffled laughter in some rooms and children running around. Many families occupied some of the rooms here, although there was also a decent amount of college students here too. The hallway's paint was slightly chipping and the rug underneath me was an appealing green with mystery stains all over. I don't want to know what any of those could be, it didn't help that it smelled like feet in here. The straightforward path led to one of the many rooms on the second level, 'Room 103'.

Reaching out a hand and lifted towards the door to knock only to pull back once I realized my hand was trembling from all the pent-up emotions from today. What would they think if they knew I was homeless? They're already not living in the most comfortable of places to begin with so—

"Oh Aaron, what are you doing here?" A voice cut my thoughts off as said room door opened to reveal Daniel standing in the doorway. His hair was damp and dawned a towel around his neck, a white T-shirt, and gray sweatpants on.

The design on his shirt managed to draw the first laugh out of me all day. "Cute shirt Danny."

Snickering, I reached out to tug on the hem of his shirt to see the design in all of its comedic glory. The design on display was a black bear drinking a cup of coffee with the historical quote, "I Desbear Mornings."

Daniel's eyes glanced down at his attire and lightly slapped my groping hands away as he snickered at me in response. "I would have dressed more presentable if I knew you were coming. Come inside."

He grasped my hand and led me inside his room, and I took the chance to nosily look around at everything. Despite being here before, it felt different this time after our kiss at that party a while ago. "Well, I don't have a home anymore… I didn't know what to do." The anxiety that left momentarily returned in a flash as the explanation flooded out of me like a faucet of emotions. "Nate told our parents that we kissed! I-I didn't know what to do or where to go?! They didn't even let me take anything; they threw me out like I meant nothing to them!" My voice cracked as the tears formed in my eyes as I fell onto my knees sobbing. "It hurts so much, my brother lied to me! My parents never even gave me a chance to explain! I have no food, no phone, no money, and I don't know what to--"

Daniel's arms quickly circled me and brought me into a warm embrace, a place that felt like... home. This was where I needed to be now, with someone who cared for me like no one else ever had.

"I am so sorry Aaron! This should not have happened to you, but you want to know something?"

The sudden question caught my attention as his grip slackened and pulled away slightly so our eyes could meet. "The reason why I'm here is because my family kicked me out too." He brought his hand up and used his fingers to gently brush away my tears as he continued. "My mother was not exactly the most responsible person while growing up. She mainly spent money on alcohol and eventually, it led to me being sent to live with my grandparents since my father left her for another woman. Once I started getting interested in dating, I found myself having an interest in all types of people, not any specific gender. Once I brought it up to them, they told me I couldn't live with them anymore, they labeled me a sexual deviant and never spoke to me again after that." Despite how tragic his story was, he did not show an ounce of sadness or anger in his eyes. The only emotion I could discern was the loving gaze he held as he combed his fingers through my hair.

"You cannot let their opinion of you define who you are. Of course, I wish it didn't unfold the way it did, but I am not going to let them make me feel ashamed of who I am, nor should you. This place here can be your new home, Aaron, with me."

That one sentence alone made me fall in love with him all over again. How was I so blessed to meet someone as perfect as Daniel? From his response, I placed my hands on his cheeks and started littering his handsome face with many kisses so he could know how much love my heart contained for him and him alone.

After the onslaught of affection, I regrettably pulled away from him and brushed my thumb lightly against his cheek, slowly dragging down to his lips causing a smile to creep onto my face. "I think I just fell in love with you again."

Daniel's eyes glanced down to my lips momentarily, something that didn't go unnoticed by the observant eyes developed over time. His hands attempted to affectionately coil around my waist before the wounds from that belt assault throbbed in response. The pained groan, unfortunately, managed to escape as my form quivered to attempt to ease the burning aftermath from earlier.

"What's wrong? Are you hurt?" As his hands attempted to lift the damp shirt concealing the wounds to inspect the extent of the injuries I quickly stood up. "No no, I'm okay really! I was just a little surprised by your boldness!"

The unconvinced look on Daniel's face was apparent, without facing him the piercing stare was felt. The sound of clothes rustling before the visual surroundings turned into pitch darkness momentarily and suddenly became cold in the living room.

"What the hell?! I did not consent to this!" Daniel removed the shirt from previously hiding my battered back and waist as I attempted and failed to cover the injuries with my hands. Concerning others with trivial things like this was something I was never fond of doing. Cowards cannot handle the pain from minor injuries like these is what Dad instilled from the beginning, no such thing as a strong man who sheds tears. "You have welts! First, you are going to shower then I will patch you up."

Before I could retort back, Daniel's hand clasped over my mouth, muffling any attempt to verbally counter, and dragged us both into his bathroom to clean me up. "Stay here, I'm going to give you some of my clothes. I'll dry your wet clothes for you too, honey." He forced me to sit down on the toilet as he fetched a spare change of clothes to replace my wet attire. Silently pouting Daniel neatly folded a fresh outfit for me as he prepared a warm bath, adding Epsom salt for the inflamed welts. "Stop pouting like a child, after your bath we will watch a movie together. How does that sound?"

This beautiful man before shined like a sun with how much love radiated off him each moment we were together. That ability of his consumed me with adoration and the need to shield him from the horrors of living. Before he could leave the bathroom, my hand grasped his shirt as I pulled him back to place a kiss on his lips. A mischievous smirk formed at the flushed surprised look that was plastered on his face.

"Oh, did I surprise you? That's what you get for being so irresistible, *honey*."

Blowing a kiss, I shut the door behind me to relax and vanquish the filth that was covering me. The bath was so pleasant I almost didn't want the moment to end, being surrounded by the comforting invisible steam wafting in the air laced with the welcomed smell of lavender. The pleasant accommodations were starting to cause another foreign feeling to develop. Gratitude was the only emotion that could be felt at that moment, despite how euphoric it may be it must end. Once the dirty water was drained from the tub and I finished dressing into the provided clothing I reunited with Daniel in the living room, we sat down to watch the anticipated movie together.

The scene before brought a sparkle of excitement into my previously vacant eyes. Daniel splayed out a variety of snacks onto the coffee table in front of the couch and a couple of DVD cases, presumably deciding on which movie would be most entertaining. Pillows and a large blanket were laid on top of the couch alongside Daniel.

"Hey, how was your bath?"

I sat next to Daniel and tiredly draped my arms around his with lidded eyes and let out a small yawn in response. "Perfect."

As I made myself comfortable, Daniel arose from the couch and crouched in front of his DVD player. "So which movie do you want to watch? Wanna watch Dragon Warrior Z, Kidney Explosion, or Love Me Like Wine?"

Pondering over the equally interesting and amusing options, horror was always the go-to, especially at night. "As tempting as Dragon Warrior Z is, Kidney Explosion is the pick tonight!"

Nodding his head in agreement, Daniel inserted the disk into the DVD player and sat back down beside me as the movie slowly began. This place was *home*, not just for me, but for both of us. Home is a place where you can feel accepted, loved, and cared for by someone you cherish with your whole being. That place was something I finally gained, after fleeing from the Clayfield family like a prisoner. This place had become our little sanctuary, the environment where both of us could be ourselves.

Daniel pulled away, adjusting the pink blanket to better encapsulate my cold body. "See how talking about your problems makes them better?" His snarky remark may have been slightly irritating, but he was right.

Nodding in agreement and letting out an exhausted yawn before responding, "Yes, you're right like always. Now can we go back to bed? It's cold out here."

Shuffling over hurriedly as Daniel opened the sliding patio door for us to enter—our shared bedroom. Both of our exhausted bodies collapsed onto the plush blankets and snuggled up close to each other to regain warmth. Daniel quietly muttered something.

"You know, we should form a band together. You, Me, and Lillie? How does that sound? I'll play my killer-ass guitar while you can drum your heart out?"

Quietly pondering the thought for a moment, I opened my eyes to meet his blue eyes staring back at me, no humor present in his demeanor. Smiling at the image of the three of us touring around the state and sharing his passion for music around the world made my heart swell.

"Hell yes, that sounds amazing!"

Sitting up and grabbing his phone to send a quick text to Lillie before we both allowed the lulling dreamland to take us away to our peaceful slumber, overjoyed to start this new journey together.